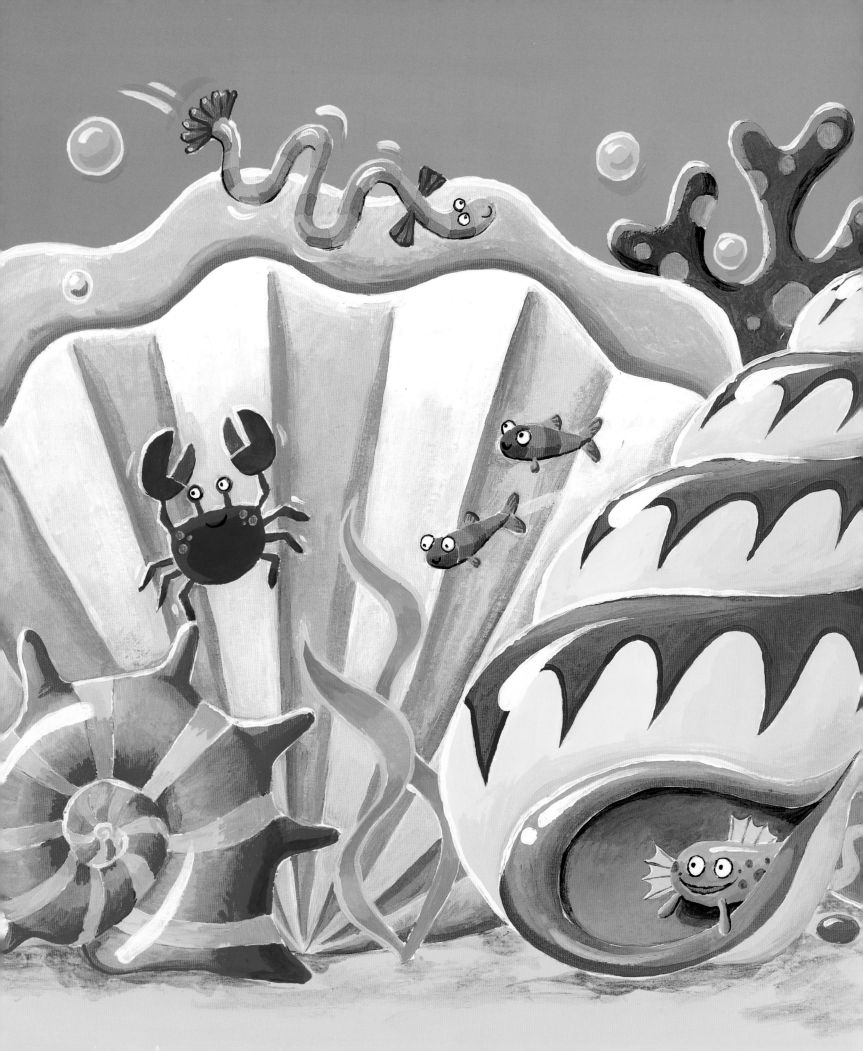

To my friend, Nick

tiger tales
5 River Road, Suite 128, Wilton, CT 06897
This edition published in the United States 2018
First published in the United States 2005
Originally published in Great Britain 2005
by Little Tiger Press
Text and illustrations copyright © 2005 Ruth Galloway
ISBN-13: 978-1-68010-086-0
ISBN-10: 1-68010-086-6
Printed in China
LTP/1400/2005/0917
All rights reserved
10 9 8 7 6 5 4 3 2 1

For more insight and activities, visit us at www.tigertalesbooks.com

Clumsy
Crab

by Ruth Galloway

tiger tales

Nipper the crab didn't like his huge, clumsy claws at all. Snip, snap! Clip, clap! No matter what he did, they always got in the way.

None of his friends had clumsy claws.
He wished he had tickly arms like Octopus, or
tentacles like Sea Jelly, or even flippety fins
like Turtle and the fish.

One day, Nipper was playing
catch-the-bubble with his friends.

POP!

His clumsy claws
burst the bubble!

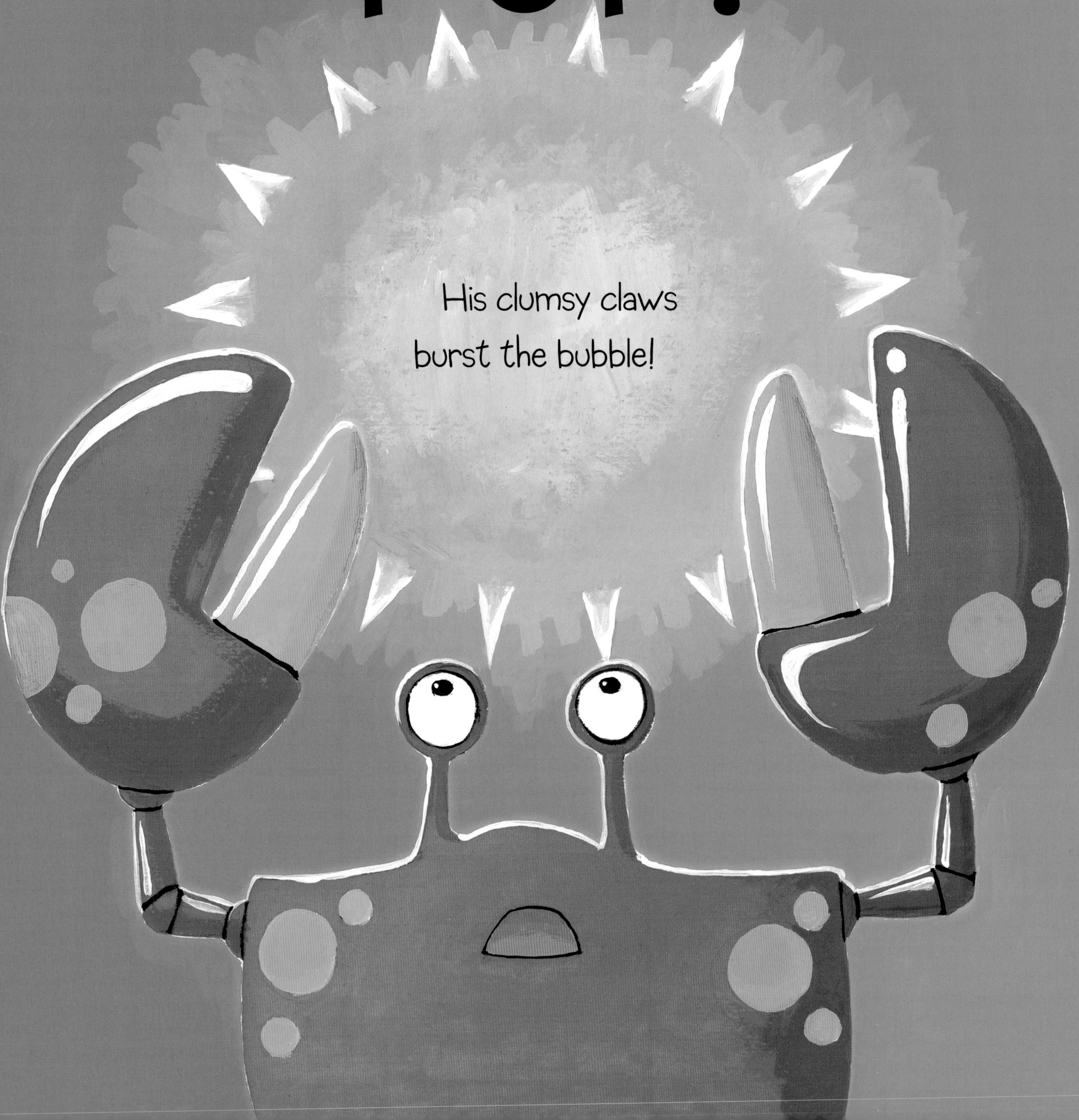

They couldn't play
that game anymore. So they
played tag instead.

Nipper scuttled off sideways,
but one of his clumsy claws got in the way.

Nipper slipped and stumbled,
tripped and tumbled, until . . .

. . . he was buried up to his eyes
in sand. Turtle came to dig him out.

Everyone decided to play hide-and-seek. Nipper climbed into a big clamshell and pulled it shut.

It was the perfect
hiding place until . . .

SMASH!

. . . Nipper's clumsy claws shattered
the shell into hundreds of tiny pieces.
"Ouch!" he cried. "Help!"

Sea Jelly picked up
the pieces of shell.

"If I didn't have these clumsy claws,
I wouldn't break everything, and I'd be good
at hide-and-seek," said Nipper.

"Don't worry, Nipper," said the others. "We'll
hide, and you can find us."

Nipper counted to ten,
then set off to find his friends.
He scuttled through the
sand . . . and found Turtle.

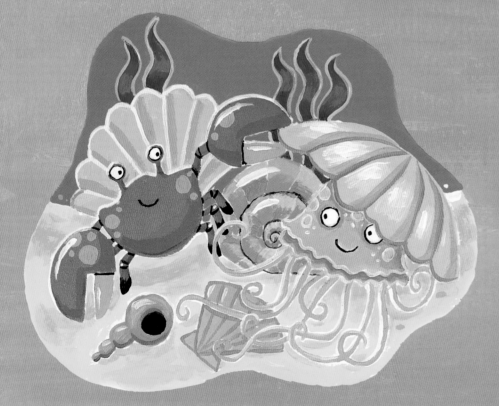

He shuffled
under the shells . . .
and found Sea Jelly.

And he searched up and down, and in
and out, and all around the rocks . . .

but he couldn't find
Octopus anywhere.

Suddenly, everyone heard a cry.
Octopus was tangled up tightly
in some seaweed!

"Help!"

Octopus squirmed and wiggled and wriggled and jiggled. Turtle and Sea Jelly tried to help, but the knots just got tighter and tighter.

Nipper had an idea.

Nipper snipped at the seaweed
with his claws. Faster and faster Nipper
danced around the clump of seaweed,
snipping and snapping, clipping and clapping!

His claws moved quickly, slashing and slicing, shredding and dicing, until the sea was filled with tiny pieces of swirling seaweed.

Octopus was finally free!
"Thank you, Nipper! You're a clever crab!"
he cheered. Nipper waved his claws happily.
At last he knew how useful they could be.

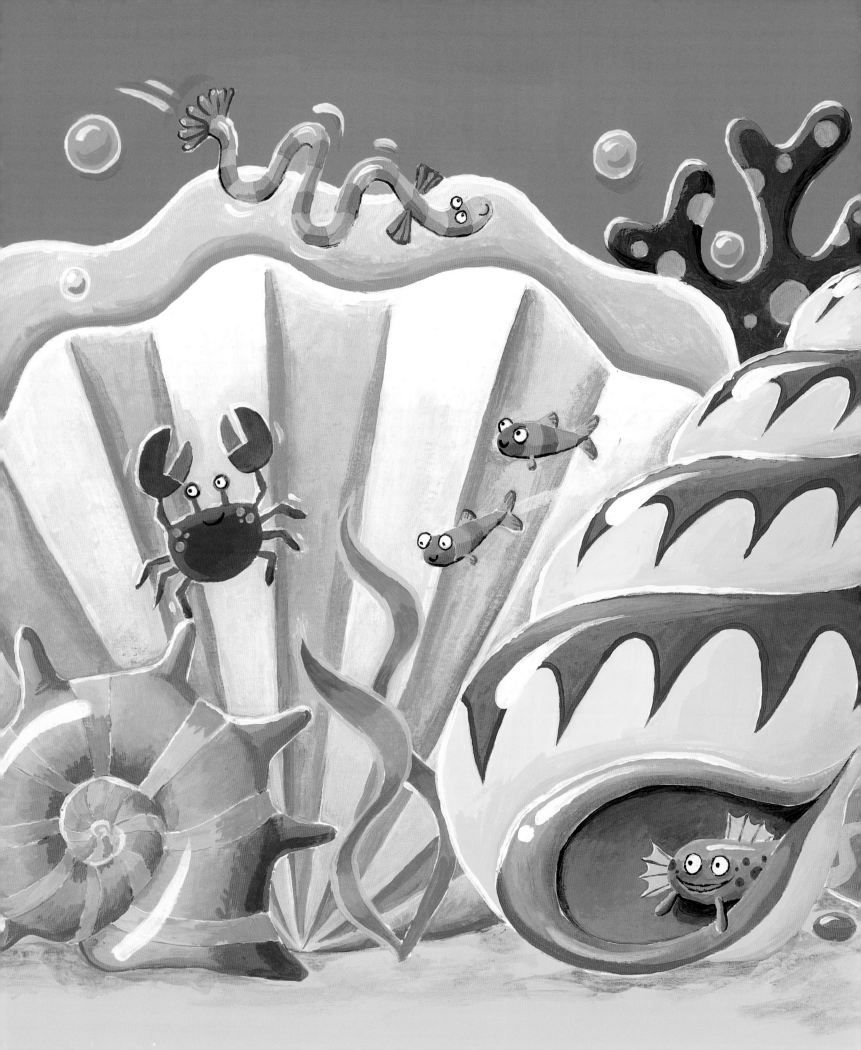

Ruth Galloway studied art in
school but is essentially self-taught.
She knew she was going to be
an artist from the age of eight and
is now a successful illustrator of
a number of picture books.

Ruth is a trained aerobics instructor,
and in her spare time, she enjoys
cooking and gardening. She is married
with two children and lives in
Berkshire, England.